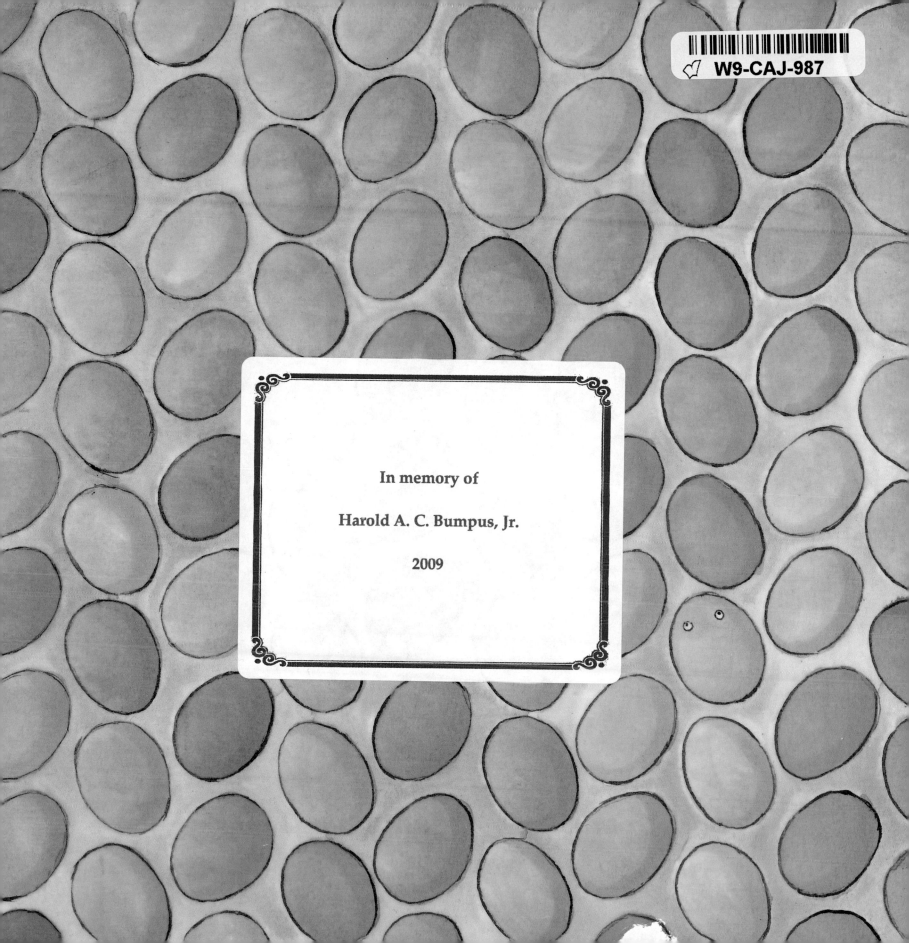

To Tony

THIS IS A BORZOI BOOK PUBLISHED BY ALFRED A. KNOPF

Copyright © 2002 by Mini Grey

Published in the United States by Alfred A. Knopf, an imprint of Random House Children's Books, a division of Random House, Inc., New York.
Originally published in 2002 in Great Britain by Jonathan Cape, an imprint of Random House Children's Books.

Knopf, Borzoi Books, and the colophon are registered trademarks of Random House, Inc.

Visit us on the Web! www.randomhouse.com/kids

Educators and librarians, for a variety of teaching tools, visit us at www.randomhouse.com/teachers

Library of Congress Cataloging-in-Publication Data
Grey, Mini.
Egg drop / Mini Grey. — 1st American ed.
p. cm.
Originally published: Great Britain : Jonathan Cape, 2002.
Summary: Tragedy strikes when an egg, eager to fly like birds, airplanes, and insects, steps off of a tall tower.
ISBN 978-0-375-84260-3 (trade) — ISBN 978-0-375-94260-0 (lib. bdg.)
[1. Eggs—Fiction. 2. Flight—Fiction.] I. Title.
PZ7.G873Eg 2009
[E]—dc22
2008024534

MANUFACTURED IN MALAYSIA
July 2009
10 9 8 7 6 5 4 3 2 1
First American Edition

egg
drop

Mini Grey

ALFRED A. KNOPF
NEW YORK

The Egg was young.
It didn't know much.
We tried to tell it,
but of course it didn't listen.

If only it had waited.

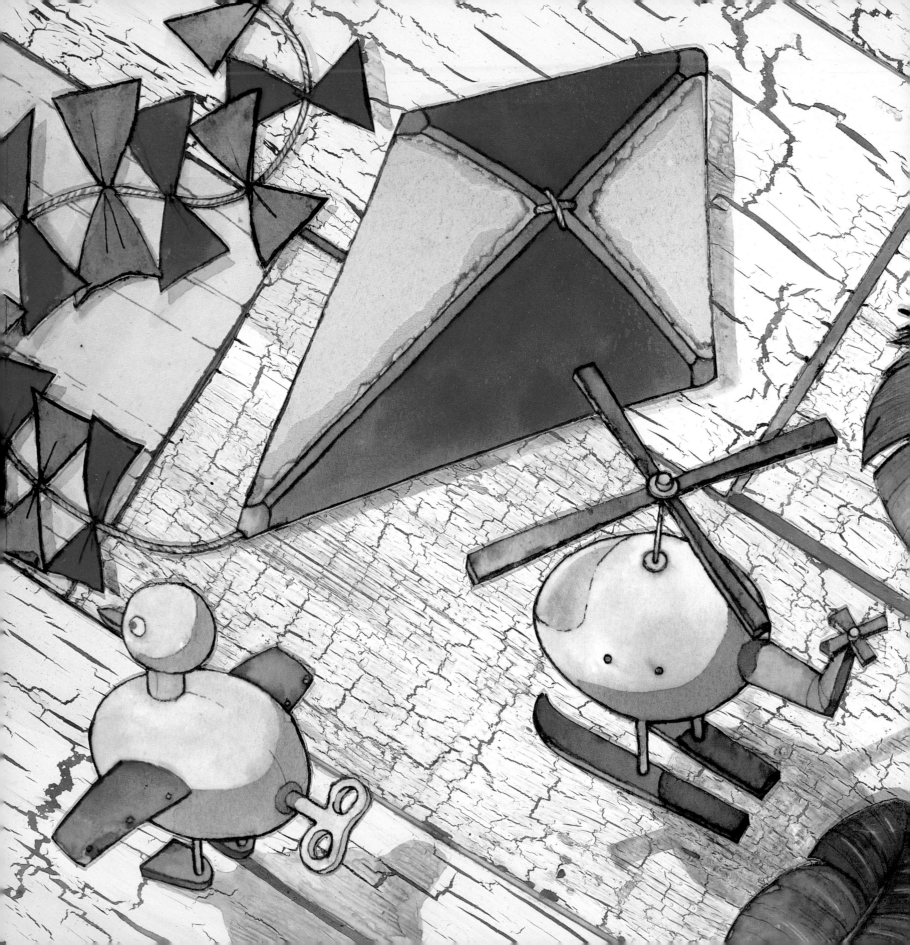

Here is the story of the Egg that wanted to fly.

The Egg had always loved looking up,
seeing birds and balloons,
airplanes and insects,
helicopters and bats and clouds.

The Egg wanted to fly with them.
It dreamed of ways to fly.

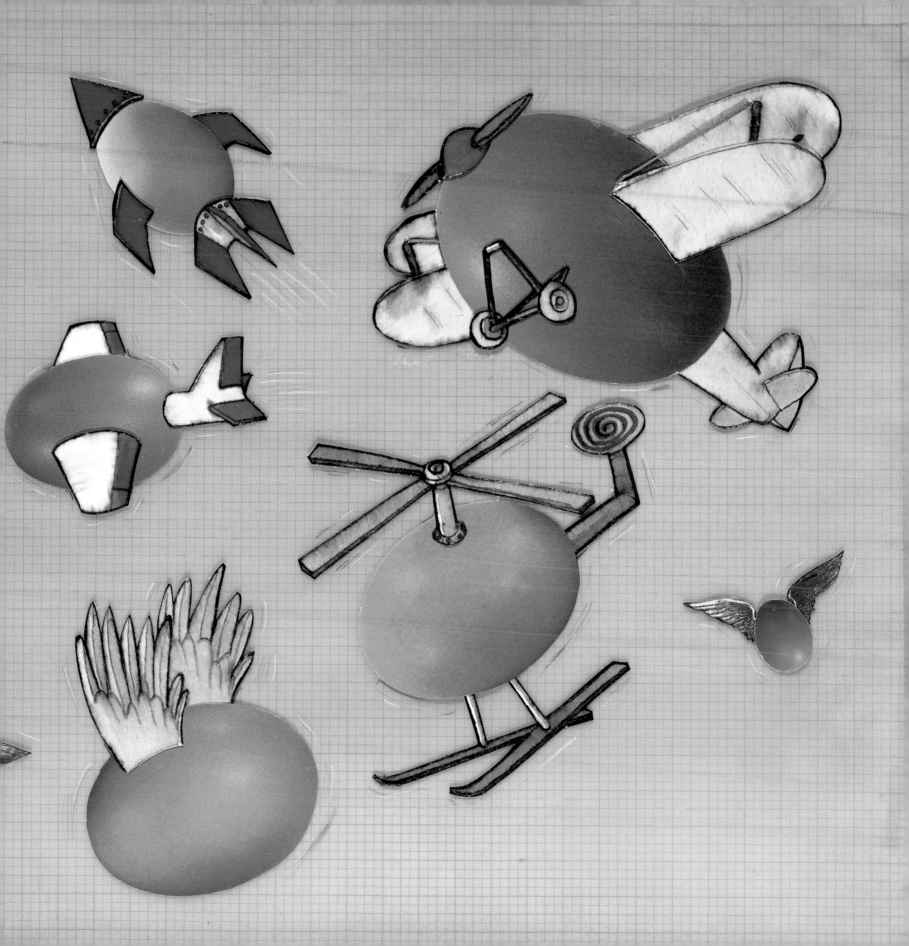

But the Egg was young.
It didn't know much about flying
(and it didn't know anything
about aerodynamics
or Bernoulli's principle).

BERNOULLI'S PRINCIPLE

faster-moving air
LOW PRESSURE

HIGH PRESSURE
slower-moving air

LIFT

Fig. 86 : The Hindenburg, which was destroyed by fire at Lakehurst,
succeeded by the LZ130

It just knew that it
had to get up high.

There was
a very tall tower
made of bricks
on a hill.
Inside there were
583 stone steps.

AN OF THE TOWER

The Egg climbed
to the top.

The Egg was in the clouds.
A bird flew past.
The Egg squeezed its eyes shut.
It drew a deep breath.
It took a step into space.

There was an enormous egg rush.

The Egg opened its eyes and saw
friends in the air, felt sky blasting past.

But the Egg
was not flying.

It was falling.

It took us a while to clean up the mess.

Band-Aids

string

sticky tape

We tried to put the Egg back together again,

sewing

chewing gum

nails

and

screws

tomato soup

but nothing really worked and shells don't heal.

The Egg was young.
It didn't listen.
If only it had waited.

FARM NEWS

EGG DROP!

THE TRAGIC end of a local egg was discovered yesterday at the base of the Very Tall Tower. The egg was found to be irreparably broken and rapidly losing albumen. Emergency services were called immediately by local poultry but all attempts at resuscitation failed. When questioned about the egg's unlucky demise, a witness reportedly commented: "The egg was young. It didn't listen. If only it had waited." When pressed to comment further the witness merely shrugged its wings and waddled slowly away. Police have asserted that there is no suspicion of fowl play.

TOO YOUNG....the egg that wanted to fly

For further information about how to make good use of broken eggs turn to our Cookery Section on page 23 Recipes in our special feature include *Oeufs en Cocotte* and *Egg Pie*, but we also preview extracts from *Cooking Eggs for Invalids*, a new book by Celia

Luckily, the Egg was not wasted.

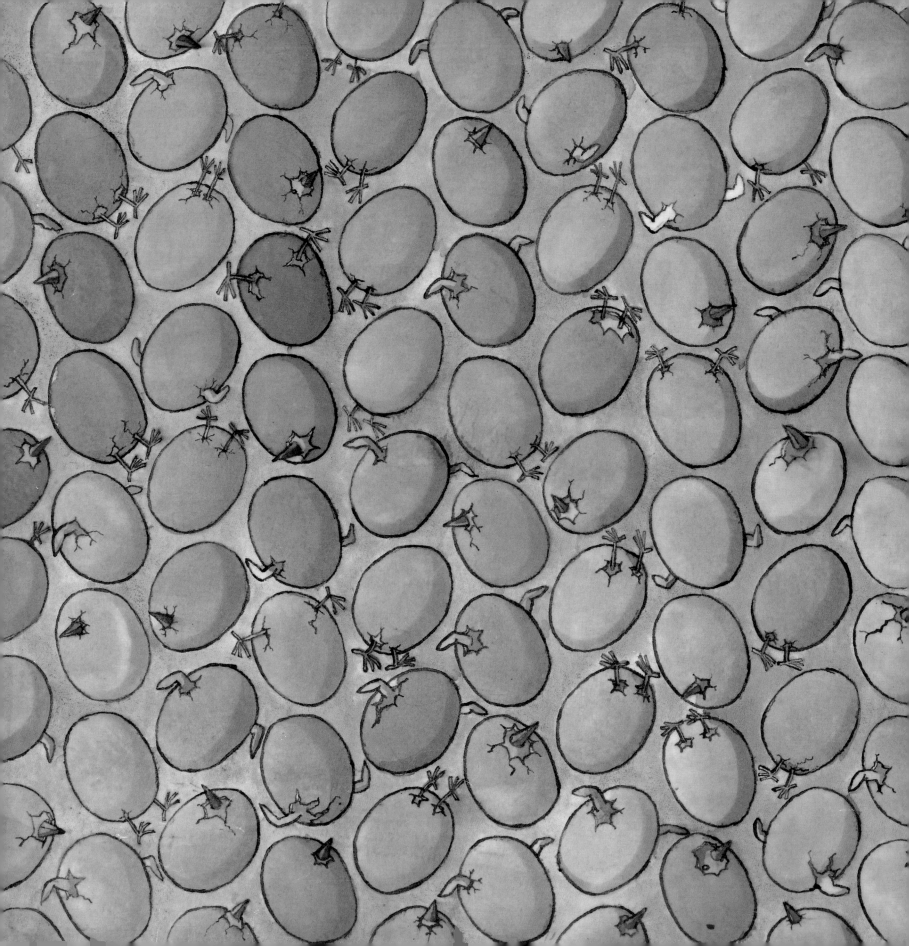